QUEEN OF THE SKY

To: Lizzie

sorry in advance :‿

ky
venn

♡

QUEEN OF THE SKY
A LEGEND OF THE PAINTED SKIES PREQUEL

KY VENN

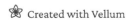

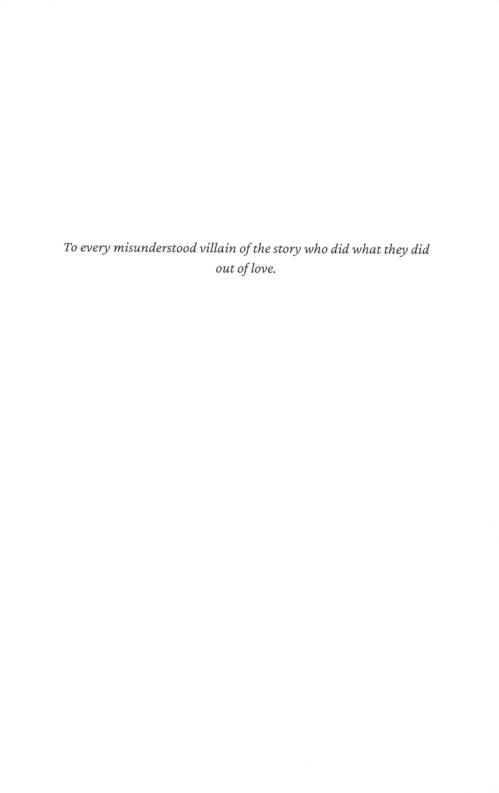

To every misunderstood villain of the story who did what they did out of love.

"Moon dust in your lungs, stars in your eyes, you are a child of the cosmos, a queen of the sky."

— UNKNOWN

A NOTE TO THE READER

Queen of the Sky is a prequel novel for the Legends of the Painted Skies series, set in a time before the events of the first book, a full length novel, to come.

WARNING

The story you are about to embark on is not a happy one. It is weaved with pain, and chaos, and destruction. This is the story of how the Goddess of Chaos came crashing down.

This book contains material that is intended for a mature audience and may not be suitable for some readers such as: open door sexual scenes, discussion of death, violence, and murder. This is not a book with a happy ending, and is a villain origin story.

Proceed at your own risk.

I

Her life was filled with nothing but mayhem, tragedy, and bitterness. She was the Goddess of chaos and disaster, after all. Aella Othonos sat perched on a steep, rocky cliff. It was part of the largest mountain in the Morrian territory. The elevation made it easy to spot her unknowing prey. They all moved quickly, with excitement in every step. As if the work they did in their village was the best thing they could ever see themselves doing. The anger that always sat dormant in her belly began to bubble up.

What pathetic little creatures.

How they disgusted her; with their cheery attitudes and smiles that blinded her like the rays of the sun. Her eyebrows were in a permanent scowl; always resting in discontent, but especially when she found herself watching these silly humans. A smirk curled on one side of her face as she held her magic weapon in the palm of her hand: one blow of her ebony dust and the entire village would explode in an uproar. It's what she lived for, what she dreamed about, what she hungered for daily.

Whilst it may not look like much, the glittery substance that flowed from her hands, its effects had the potential to be deadly and catastrophic. A single breath of air from her lips in a human's direction and they'd crumple to the ground and if they weren't killed on impact, they'd wish they had been.

Aella was born thirsting for chaos. She had grown up this way, and would always be this way. She was also raised surrounded by Gods and Goddesses who taught her to despise humans. Though they may have never spoken of their hatred out loud, they made it clear with their attitudes and actions. They lived separated from humans, their home in the Sky, and the humans on the ground, but it didn't mean their paths didn't cross every once in a while. Occasionally a pesky human decided to try their luck against the mighty beings of Verus, and set foot into their home. It didn't last long before one of the various beings catapulted their powers towards the intruder, and extinguished their life like the flame of a candle. Very few humans sought out the Gods and Goddesses of the Sky as Aella sought out the humans, but alas, she couldn't rain chaos on her own home; the Gods who ruled over it frowned upon that.

Instead, every once in a while, she snuck down to Earth and satisfied her deep desire for causing turmoil. It's what she was good at, and she knew that sooner or later it was going to catch up with her, and the Gods of the Sky were going to tether her to the Verus, never to leave again. It was only a matter of time, and she could feel the impending imprisonment crawling closer and closer with each day.

Rarely did something stir her cold, black, heart. It took quite the effort to cause it to feel anything, but the thought of being banished to Verus for eternity made the organ ache. It wasn't so much the thought of not being able to come down and torment the humans. It was more about the ability to come and go as she pleased; her freedom. That possibility would be stripped away from her, and just the thought of it was almost too much to bear. Once she was contained to the Sky, she knew the ban would never be lifted.

Aella could imagine her father's anger at her leaving the grounds and sneaking away, the possibility of her existence being found out. They were myths and legends, but nobody ever could confirm they were real. She knew this wouldn't last forever though. One day the humans would confirm their existence. One would sneak in to Verus and live to tell the tale, and then they'd all begin to do the same. Soon after they'd begin to ask for things, and want things only a mighty being could give. Once one came, more would follow. Then the selfish, petty humans would take from them and make foolish demands.They'd quickly learn, however, that the people of Verus were not afraid to strike them down where they stood. The only reason humans and the Sky Gods lived in harmony was because the mortals hadn't discovered Verus. The Gods weren't meant to be put on display.

If her father could see her now, tiptoeing her way down the hidden stairs to Earth, he would be sitting on his throne, lightning crackling from his fingertips, while her mother looked at her with disappointment shining in her eyes. That was another thing she couldn't bear. Disappointing her parents.

She was loved as a child and raised in a good and happy home. Her parents were in love; bearing seven children total, including herself. Their house was always full of noise and excitement. But as her siblings aged and moved away, the

3

chaos dimmed. Followed closely by her happiness. She was the youngest of Ezros and Roena's children, and soon they would force her to move into her own place. She supposed maybe this was why she continued to risk coming down to Earth. It was a way to rebel, because she didn't want to leave her childhood home. It was a lot easier to cause chaos when she didn't have her own home to worry about and maintain.

Many would look at Aella and be surprised she came from such a happy family. Her gifts were chaos and discord. Most believed there wasn't a happy bone in her body. Especially when they looked at her. Her eyes were the color of blood, compared to the golden eyes of her parents and siblings. Her father told her stories growing up that when she came out of her mother's womb, she opened her eyes and the healers thought something was wrong. But as she grew, everyone realized there was no mistake; the crimson orbs matched her very soul.

Cold and deadly.

Where she had the eyes of death, and pin straight black hair, her siblings complexions were full of life and joy. Honey blonde, strawberry blonde, and fawn brown hair adorned her siblings, with a handful of blue and green eyes to match. She was the ugly duckling of her family. The black sheep. The freak of nature.

But despite their differences when it came to looks, the only thing that thawed her cold soul was her family. Nothing else came close, and nothing else brought her happiness. Well, besides when she was creating a mess in others' lives. Besides the typical sibling banter, they never treated her as if she was any different. Although deep down she knew goodness flowed through their veins, while darkness coursed through hers.

A crunch of a branch behind her brought her out of her thoughts.

What a wonderful surprise.

"Turn around slowly," a deep male voice said behind her, and she heard the distinct sound of a bow string being pulled. She could *smell* the human before she saw him. A smile crept on her lips at the opportunity presented to her before she dissipated into thin air. She'd terrified her parents when she first showed off that little trick.

Didn't see that coming, did you human?

"What do we have here?" She purred into his ear as she reappeared at his side. She took a split second to take in the man before her. With his honey-blonde hair and chocolate brown eyes he looked like every single one she'd ever seen. Nothing special.

"How did you do that witch?" He growled, turning, and backing away from her, towards the cliff. She was surprised, for only a moment, to see that he lacked fear in his eyes when he bore into her own. When she broke eye contact with him, she noticed the arrow from his bow was still pointed directly at her. But she had nothing to fear with these humans. She'd disappear before he had the chance to let his arrow fly.

"Witch, hmm? Nothing I haven't heard before. All you humans are the same," she laughed, flicking her long dark hair over her shoulder, and slowly circling him to appraise her prey. "I don't think your small brain would be able to comprehend what I'm capable of."

"Try me. You'd be surprised," he replied, one eye closed to continue to aim the arrow at her heart. "Or better yet, tell me why you were spying on my village."

The tone in his voice was the coldest she'd heard come out of a human. They didn't usually stand too long in her presence. But he remained unfazed by her appearance and not at all concerned about the small hint of her gifts that she had put on display for him.

"What an incredibly stupid human you must be," she laughed. "Standing in my presence, demanding answers to your questions from me. Don't you know who I am?"

"You look like a trespasser to me. I've seen you watching our village before. Every hunting trip I take, you're up here. Thinking nobody notices you lurking." He snarled, not flinching, or showing any outward fear.

This is impossible. He isn't fazed by me at all.

"I could end you with the snap of my fingers, and a sprinkle of my dust. You underestimate me." she said, opening her hand and releasing the sparkling black powder she'd intended for the village. She inhaled a deep breath, ready to blow destruction towards him.

"No witch, I think it's you who underestimates me."

As his last word left his lips, he released the arrow from his bow.

2

Aella was grateful at that moment for her incredible speed and immortality. Without which she'd likely be bleeding out and dead in moments. She quickly turned to smoke and the arrow sailed through her, impaling a tree behind her.

"Big mistake human," she snapped, materializing in front of him, her hand wrapped around his throat before he had a moment to blink. She began to walk slowly, lifting him easily off the ground by his throat, towards the edge of the cliff. He was taller than she was, but she made easy work carrying him with one hand. It was a steep drop off the cliff in the area the village hadn't occupied, and it would break every bone in his body, killing him instantly.

He didn't flinch as she held him over the edge, his eyes like cold steel. For a split second, she allowed herself to be caught off guard. Never had a human had the nerve to stare her dead in the eyes, unphased by the blood red ones staring back at them. She was used to her prey crumbling in fear and agony before her. She let her mask slip for just a moment, having never experienced something of this caliber before. But then she recomposed herself, refusing to be made a fool by this man.

"How does it feel?" She asked, planting her feet on the ground.

"How does what feel?" He choked out, his face turning red.

"To have your life in my hands," she sneered. "I let you go, and I feel nothing. One less human I have to look at and deal with."

"But you won't." He said, another smirk crawling over his lips.

"What makes you so sure?" She said, bringing her face close to his. She didn't take her eyes off of his, refusing to back down. She hadn't planned to kill a human herself today. No, she'd let them do that themselves. Whether accidental or not, they stupidly took each other's lives every day. But this one was grating so heavily on her nerves; it wouldn't hurt to drop him from the cliff.

"Theron?" A voice asked from behind them. Shock flooded through her. It was rare that she was caught off guard.

There were more of them?

"Not one step closer, or I drop your friend to his death," she said, not taking her eyes from Theron.

"I don't think you will," the newcomer said.

"What is with you humans and underestimating the chaos that runs through my veins?" A chuckle escaped her, but it lacked humor.

She heard the sound of swords leaving their sheaths, and more bow strings being pulled back. She was incredibly outnumbered. Although she was just one woman, she was powerful enough to take them all. But this many humans in one day? They made it too easy for her. All she'd have to do is drop this silly human from the cliff and sprinkle the others with her dust.

"Maybe not today, but I'll be back for you, my dear," Aella promised, giving Theron a quick kiss on the cheek to seal the deal of her promise. "See you later, gentlemen," she said, before disappearing into the air, leaving a trail of nothing but dust behind.

3

Theron's body slammed to the ground, causing the little bit of oxygen still left in his chest to violently leave him. He clutched his throat, glad for the oxygen returning to his lungs. He hadn't shown it on the outside, but on the inside, he had been terrified for his life. He knew she could have dropped him from the cliff, and he wouldn't have survived to tell the tale. As a warrior, he was no stranger to the possibility of death. But when it was looking him point blank in the face, nothing but an unclutching of a hand away, it was different. The rest of his clan began to move forward to approach him, but he put his hand out in front of him.

"DON'T MOVE!" Theron shouted, his voice weak but urgent. The men stopped suddenly, some nearly tripping over others. He silently pointed up, at the black glittering dust sparkling in the wind as it slowly fell to the ground, like ash from a fire. "RUN!"

The men turned without a thought, never having doubted Theron and his commands. He'd been leading these men for years now, and they never turned their back on him. He couldn't help but feel gratitude for every one of them, especially in a moment when all of their lives depended on it. He used his tunic and covered his mouth and his nostrils so the dust didn't invade his lungs. It wouldn't work entirely, but the effect of the dust would be lessened.

Theron held his breath as long as possible, but he felt the powder go through his nostrils as he was forced to inhale. Black dots filled his vision and he felt his heart pounding faster against his chest. Visions flashed before his eyes, some real and some he hoped were the effects of the wretched magical dust. Blood, birds, and death overwhelmed him.

This wasn't the first time he had felt the power of the witch's dust. She'd been haunting his village for years and had brought terror to his people. He was just a wee lad the first time he had been exposed to it. He was out helping his father in the barn and the sky had turned dark in the blink of an eye. He had never felt such terror fill his veins before. He had wet himself, and his father had come back to consciousness first. He'd found Theron laying on the barn floor, shaking, and mumbling to himself. It was the first time he remembered something of that level happening. He and his father had been lucky to have even survived an attack that severe, and to walk away with no long lasting effects. Still, Theron couldn't help but wonder if that moment coupled with a few others were what led his father to an early trip to his grave.

Ever since the first attack, the village had taken as many precautions as they could to stay safe from the witch and the damage she loved to cause. Around the clock, guards circled the village, and gas masks were given to every civilian that populated Bryxton. It worked a majority of the time, but there were those select few who lived within the village that didn't believe in the witch any longer. Some newcomers who lacked the history of seeing what she could do. Sometimes it took someone learning a lesson the hard way for it to finally sink in. It had been so long since she had attacked, or the villagers had been affected, that they stopped believing. For a while even Theron wasn't sure if she was still around and watching. But now Theron had proof that she was back. He never should have doubted it, or himself, in the first place. He had dared to hope, and that was dangerous.

He lay there on the hard ground trying to keep his composure and waiting for the wave of misery he knew was coming any moment to wash over him. He was drenched in his own sweat, nausea flooding him. His eyes were open, but he couldn't see the sky. All he could see was pitch black darkness surrounding him.

Theron wasn't sure how long he had been lying there, but the darkness started to dissipate and black spots flooded his vision again, and then it was clear. He was back to his reality, and the sky was above him once more. He sat up slowly, his head foggy, unable to focus his vision, and vomited on the ground next to him.This instance was nothing compared to the effects the potent dust used to have on him. Thanks to the many hours of practicing meditation during his training, he was able to overcome the effects at a quicker rate. The symptoms were bearable and fast to resolve. A normal human would be in the infirmary for days or weeks without the proper training to pull themselves out of the trenches.

Anything Theron could do to fight back against the witch was good enough for him.

4

It didn't take long for Aella to make it back to Verus, especially following the way of the wind. Her feet materialized first before her, and the rest of her followed behind quickly. She stopped right in front of the gates, ready to walk into her home. Tormenting the mortal had surprisingly taken a lot out of her. A bubble bath was already calling her name, and she knew her sore muscles would thank her for it later.

She wasn't sure why, but in recent years all of her havoc wreaking had caught up to her. She'd been having to take longer and longer breaks in between her visits to the village. It was beginning to take a toll, and a nagging voice in the back of her head was telling her she needed to visit the Source of Eternal Life. To take a dip in its aqua blue, cool waters, and feel her essence returned to her.

"Your father is looking for you," one of the guards at the front gate said. His expression was emotionless and stopped her in her tracks.

That's not a good sign.

"What for?" Aella asked, curiosity taking over her tone. Her father had rarely ever called for her, and when he did it wasn't directly outside of the Sky gates. She felt fear slice through her, but tried not to think too much about it. It could be nothing. But then again, it could be everything. Her emotions pinballed back and forth within her, and panic started to spread through her body, but she kept her face neutral so the guards wouldn't sense it.

"I am not privy to that information, Miss Aella," the first guard replied again. The second hadn't moved, just stared straight ahead. She refrained from rolling her eyes, hating when they called her "Miss" anything. It may be the proper etiquette when speaking to someone, but if they were going to add any title in front of her name, she'd prefer "Princess. Nevertheless, she kept the annoyance out of her reply.

"Okay then..." She said, now letting her confusion be clear in her tone. "Lead the way please."

"Pierce will lead the way for you," he replied, nodding towards the gates that were now opening, to another guard inside. He was younger than the other two at the front gates, but in an instant she recognized him. She had grown up with him, but it had been years since she'd seen him. He'd been training with the guard, which took him away from the general population for years.

There was an inactive volcano at the very top of a large mountain in Verus where the Royal guard went for training every five years that they opened up for new members to join. The first part of training was a long, exhausting six week experience. Marksmanship, endurance, mass amounts of cardio and strength training, as well as training with various weapons. In total, the new recruits spent three years on the mountain, to strengthen themselves and their minds.

At the very end, they came back stronger, determined and with a longer life span. The gift of years was one of the perks of being a part of the Royal Guard. The Gods and Goddesses couldn't have guards who were supposed to be protecting them dropping left and right like flies.

"Aella?" Pierce questioned, his tone laced with hope, and his face lighting up with recognition. He was incredibly handsome, even more so than she remembered. The years away had been good to him. His dark hair was shaggy and long, and his eyes were as blue as she remembered. When they were kids she swore she could jump into his eyes and swim through the oceanic depths of them. He had been one of the first Beings she had feelings for, but when he left, she attributed it to being a mindless youngling who didn't know any better.

Pierce was one of the only friends she had growing up and it surprised her that he had been friends with her at all. Even as a child she was intimidating to most. Sure, she was a cute kid, but the blood red eyes scared everyone who peered within them. Pierce had never shown her any fear. He approached her one day by the lake where Aella visited and played often, offered to share his toys, and they'd been friends ever since.

"Pierce!" she yelled, running at full speed and leaping into his arms. A grunt escaped him although he caught her with ease as she wrapped herself tightly around him. He returned her embrace by wrapping his arms around her and burying his face in the crook of her neck.

They stood like this for a moment before he gently set her down. He looked deeply into her eyes, and couldn't deny the nervousness that panged her to be examined by him. She wasn't sure what it was about him that caught her off guard, but for some reason he unsteadied her. Maybe it was his good looks, and how well his uniform fit him? He had changed very much from the tall, skinny boy she used to chase around the clouds. Now, he was all deep voiced and had bulging muscles. Maybe the crush her teenage self had was resurfacing, except now she could do something about it if she wanted. She wasn't a child anymore. And it was clear that he wasn't either. She snapped herself out of the dreamlike state. She could drool over his manliness privately, later.

Get it together Aella.

"How was your training?" She asked as she began to walk past him. The smell of sweat and earth filled her nostrils as she passed. He even smelled like a man now. No more did he smell like sweet candy and sunscreen.

"It was incredible. Thanks for asking!" He replied, turning on his heel and following her. "I missed home, though."

As he said this, he glanced at her. As if he was implying he missed *her*.

"Well, I'm glad you're back and in one piece," she said truthfully. He was one of her only friends besides her siblings. She had scared all of the other children away when she went to school. Since Pierce had been gone, she'd been alone. Well, not alone if you counted her time spent with her parents. And on Earth. But she realized seeing Pierce now, that she'd truly been lonely for the last several years. She was glad he was home.

He was like the ying to her yang. He balanced her out. His personality was shiny, where her's was cloaked in darkness.

"Yeah. yeah El, I'm sure you are," he joked, pushing his shoulder into hers. She laughed, for the first time in a long time. Everyone assumed she was an incredibly cruel, unhappy, dull person. But those who knew her, truly knew her, knew she was great at telling jokes. She was great to hang out with. She had feelings and love in her heart.

At least I think so.

"So do you have any idea why my father has sent for me?" She asked, hoping maybe her old friend would spill the secret behind her father's call.

"I'm sorry El," Pierce said sadly. "I don't know what he is wanting to discuss with you."

She could tell he wasn't being entirely truthful with her, which was disappointing.

"So you don't know what it's about, or you don't want to tell me?" She said, turning her hand to smoke and snaking it around his shoulder. She attempted to scare him just a little bit, maybe he'd be more compelled to tell her what she wanted to know.

"I don't know. I swear El. I know he's upset with you. That's all that I can tell you." He said, giving a small, disgusted look at the smoky hand that drifted over his shoulder. He'd never shown her fear when they were children, and he wasn't going to now. She added it to the list of things that hadn't changed about him since he's been gone.

"Fine, I guess I believe you," she teased, materializing her hand back to its solid form. She could feel his warmth on her skin, and she struggled to keep her hand around him. He was taller than her, and she had to look up at him when he spoke. She slowly removed her arm as his eyes locked with hers. She looked away and turned her focus to the clouds ahead of her.

The floors of Verus were made of clouds and stone walkways that led the way to various buildings and structures and the palace that housed the God and Goddesses. There were only ten Gods and Goddesses in power at a time. They could live forever, but many of them decided to leave their thrones in the Sky and live untethered. When this happened, new Beings who were trained all their lives would replace them. Not all the Gods and Goddesses shared the same powers when they replaced those who came before them. It kept things... interesting in Verus to say the least.

There was no human alive that had seen Verus and lived to tell the tale. If they had lived to bear witness to its wonder, they would describe many similarities to Earth. There were various trees, ponds, and animals that could be found on Earth as well as in Verus. The sun still rose and set on the land, and the moonlight still lit up the area during the nighttime. There were no clouds in Verus, because they lived above them and on them. They grew above them and with them. Clouds were wispy things rumored to be full of secrets. When the rain came down on Earth, if the humans listened closely enough, they could hear whispers in the raindrops. The clouds welcomed the Gods and Goddesses home and brought them all great comfort in their souls. The closer to the clouds, the greater their power. It's why she was weaker on Earth and had to depend on her dust. She couldn't use her smoke capabilities as easily. Just the disappearing act she had performed earlier was enough to make her light headed. No matter how similar the two landscapes might have seemed, Verus was mystical. It had a certain power in the air that one could feel vibrating in their bones.

She smiled to herself at the feeling of her chaos growing inside her, wanting to be unleashed. The power that each step on the clouds brought her. But she refused to bring any harm to her home.

"El?" Pierce said, his voice penetrating through her thoughts. They'd stopped in front of the Sky's main building.

They used it for their town hall meetings, their court proceedings, and everything in between.

"What are we doing here Pierce? Why aren't we at my house?" Aella asked, turning to face him. His face betrayed him, and she could see the sadness written there. "What the hell is going on?"

He looked deep in thought, and he opened his mouth to answer but was interrupted by a cough from behind her. Pierce's eyes flew up to the presence behind her, and she already knew - without a shadow of a doubt - it was her father. He was the highest Being here, and everyone bowed to him. He ruled over everyone and everything. Which included the guard. Her father may have known Pierce when they were growing up, but that didn't mean he wouldn't strip him of his title in an instant if he felt it was necessary.

"Father, what's going on?" Aella asked, crossing her arms over her chest. Her father towered over her, and she felt like a child all over again. She was only a fraction of his age, and he reminded her of that often. He'd been alive for thousands of years, whereas she'd only graced the Sky for a few centuries.

"We will discuss it inside," her father said. Before she could say another word, he turned and walked back through the open doors. Aella huffed before following after him, Pierce trailing at her heels. If anyone could make her feel small and powerless in her own skin it was her father. She felt like he'd see her as nothing more than a teenager forever.

"It'll all be ok El, don't worry," Pierce said, placing a hand on her shoulder. She hoped he was right, because nothing about this felt good. She was filled with worry and dread, and her chaos swirled inside her uneasily, as if it could sense the trouble ahead.

5

Aella entered the colosseum and marveled a little at the great sandstone walls and columns that towered high above her. She hadn't been here since she was a child. They often held community events of all kinds here, but she hadn't attended any for years. Without Pierce, it was pointless. She knew she'd be mocked when she walked through the door, and that meant it was harder to control the storm that raged inside of her. No one was ever brave enough to say anything directly to her, but she heard the whispers behind her back. She had no time for fun and games or parties and alcohol. It made her seem strange and out of touch, but she preferred chaos to organization and plans. It was safer for everyone, anyway if she didn't attend. Less of a chance for her internal fury to come to the surface.

Her father sat at a wooden table in the open of one of the larger rooms, and light flooded in from above. It didn't rain in Verus. Unless the water Goddess had a bad day or the crops needed watering, of course. They had to grow their food somehow.

Her father wasn't seated alone, however. Her mother sat by his side, her head bowed, as if she was saying a prayer, or sleeping. Neither would surprise Aella. What did surprise her was seeing her mother here at all. Her father usually handled any matters of importance by himself.

"Aella, please have a seat," her father said sternly, his hands clasped on the table in front of him. "We have something to discuss."

She slowly walked towards the table, unsure what was happening. She pulled a chair back from the table and sat at the opposite end of her father. She felt small in front of him, and was afraid to meet his eyes. Again, she felt small and like a child being scolded.

"Where have you been today Aella?" Her father asked calmly. Her head immediately snapped up. Had he known she had traveled below to Earth and visited the humans? Is that what this was about? She knew, although his tone was calm, that she shouldn't be fooled that he wasn't seething with anger at whatever she had done to upset him.

"I was taking a walk around the garden," Aella lied effortlessly. She'd had a lot of practice over the years, so she hoped her skillfulness wouldn't fail her now. She locked her gaze on his, hoping he couldn't see the deceit behind her eyes. It was treason to communicate with the humans. It compromised their existence. Humans weren't supposed to know the Gods and Goddesses existed. It was like vampires, werewolves, and fairies. No one could know of their existence, or they could end up being hunted *out* of existence. Though a mortal would have a hell of a time trying to kill any of the inhabitants of Verus.

"You dare *lie* to me Aella?" her father boomed, a fire raging in his eyes. He was beyond angry, and she knew then and there that he was well aware of exactly where she had been.

"Father, please don't be angry with me," she begged, trying to persuade him to take it easy on her. Who knew what consequences awaited her?

Aella ran everything that she did today through her head, trying to figure out where she may have slipped up. She'd been down to Earth hundreds of times and, besides the very first time all those years ago, she'd never been caught. She'd never been brought in for questioning or punishment. She was stealthy with her escape down through the clouds.

"Angry? Oh, I am not angry, Aella." Her father chuckled darkly. "I'm furious, and incredibly disappointed with you. You know better than to go down to Earth. Especially after your last warning."

She wanted to sink into her chair and disappear. He was right, this wasn't the first time she had broken his rules, and technically committed treason, by roaming down to Earth. She did it as a way to rebel, not to betray the entire race of Higher Beings. She just wanted to stay at home with her parents. She didn't want to expose, and possibly be the destruction of, her people's existence. Going down to Earth and wreaking havoc was soothing to her, and she bit back her tongue when she thought about snapping at him about it. Would he rather her stay in Verus constantly, and wreak havoc on her own people? She had to have some kind of outlet for the chaos that ran through her veins. If she didn't release it, it would eat her from the inside. It was like asking a bird not to sing. It just wasn't in her nature.

"I have dealt with your heathenish behavior long

enough. If I don't take action, people will think I've grown soft. They will think anyone can do as they please without consequence." her father explained.

She looked to her mother, waiting for her to step in and say something, but she stayed silent, refusing to meet anyone at the table's eyes. She looked back to where Pierce stood by the doors, whose gaze on her was heartbreaking.

"What are you saying, Father?" Aella asked, her voice shaking and betraying her courage.

"By the power vested in me by the Circle, I hereby banish you, Aella Othonos, from the Sky. You will be stripped of your powers, and no longer allowed to have contact with any of the other Sky inhabitants."

She heard his words. She knew she did, but she couldn't believe them. She wanted to cry and scream, but she just sat in the chair, shocked beyond words. This couldn't be happening. She couldn't be forced to leave her home. All she had been trying to do was stay with her family, not leave them for eternity. She was trying to keep their people safe. She had desperately needed an outlet. Now her chaos magic had cost her everything. She fought fiercely to hold back the tears that threatened to spill when her siblings's faces, and her nieces and nephews's faces flashed through her mind. That was all she would have of them anymore: memories.

"You will live on Earth, as a human, with a normal life span. Your centuries won't affect that. You'll be sent with twenty years already gone. You will be what you despise, as punishment for treason against your people."

She did scream then, at the pain that coursed through her body. She felt like her soul was being ripped from her. As if she'd never be whole again. She looked at her mother and saw tears flooding down her cheeks. He was taking the one thing from her that made her whole. Without it, she knew she'd truly fall apart, never to be put back together again.

"Mother! Please do something!" She yelled, but her mother just squeezed her eyes shut and forced the sound of her daughter's screams out of her ears. Aella tried to turn her head to see Pierce, but he wasn't looking at her either. The boy she'd known her entire life, the one she knew now she had loved. Every letter she received from him in those three years he was gone, signed 'love Pierce' had made her heart ache and skip a beat. Now his refusal to fight for her caused her heart to plummet into her stomach. Had he ever loved her at all?

"Pierce, please help me," she said, her voice barely above a whisper. He mimicked her mother's movements, squeezing his eyes shut, tears making their way down his face. She turned her eyes back towards the front of the table, and her father's stare was stern.

Nobody is going to save me from my fate.

The pain of her powers being stripped was almost too much for her to bear. She had never known pain before. Her immortality and speed of healing had protected her against that. All she'd ever felt was the minor pain of a scraped knee. Or the sting of a bee when she accidentally stepped on one in the garden. This was truly like nothing she had ever felt. It was as if her body was being ripped in two. Her skin felt as if it was on fire. Her eyes felt like they could pop out of her head, and her skull threatened to shatter into a million pieces from the pain. It was as if flames of red hot fire were licking her muscles, and she would have given anything to turn it off.

"Father, please stop this," she begged, her tears betraying her now.

24

"I can't Aella. You know that."

His response was the last thing she heard before her vision faded, and darkness consumed her.

ARE THOSE CHICKENS?

Aella awoke with a start, her clothes clinging to her skin and soaked through with sweat. She took in her surroundings and knew she wasn't in Verus anymore. She was dressed in an old, ratty dress she had seen the servants wear at home. Her long dark hair was in tangles, and she could feel how puffy her face was from her tears. She had awoken on a small cot, and the smell of dirt, hay, and manure assaulted her nose. She'd never smelled anything like it, and she leaned over the side of the bed to vomit. Her stomach rumbled once she had emptied its contents, and she realized it meant she was hungry. Another thing she'd never had to deal with feeling before. She was overwhelmed with all of these new experiences, and it made her stomach turn again at the overwhelming wave of emotion. When she looked around her, the ground was bare and covered in freshly laid hay. The only window in the room was caked in a thick layer of dirt. Rays of light filtered through a moth-eaten curtain. Those that could get through the dirty window, anyhow.

Aella gathered her bearings and was hit with the reality of the harsh sentencing her father had passed upon her. She'd been cast from the Sky like a fallen angel. She had no idea how humans lived, and now she was supposed to live among them. She had no idea how to handle hunger, tiredness, and pesky emotions. The humans were insignificant worms, and she loathed them. She was one of the strongest Goddesses of her generation, and now she was powerless. She didn't have time for these things to hold her back from her true potential. The longer she was powerless, the weaker her powers would be when she got back to Verus. Which she would. Her father couldn't keep her down here forever. It wasn't fair, and she'd be damned before she accepted being tossed aside this way.

Aella quietly pulled back the flimsy covers and looked at her bedside table, which in reality was just an old wooden barrel. A metal pitcher of water, an empty cup, and a note lay there, waiting to be read. She took a deep breath and willed herself to pick up the paper and read it. Instantly when her eyes grazed the written words, she recognized the handwriting.

> *Aella,*
>
> *I've left some coins here for you. That should give you a night or two at this inn until you find work. It was the best I could do. I'm sorry it had to come to this. You've let your father and I down, as well as your people. You should consider yourself lucky that your father didn't take away your memories and your ability to think or speak of us at all. He trusts that you'll make the right choice and not endanger your family more than you already have.*
>
> *I hope this teaches you the lesson you need to learn. I wish you didn't need to learn things the hard way. We will miss you, and we will always love you, no matter how else we may be feeling my darling girl. You*

will always be my little Chaos, no matter how far you may be. Please don't be angry at your father. He had to make a hard choice to do what was best for Verus. You must learn to control the destruction that is weaved through your heart.

May the Sky be with you,
Mother

TEARS PRICKED HER EYES. HAD HER FATHER KNOWN HER MOTHER had done this? How did she even have human money? Her mother's loving words hit her harder than she'd ever felt before, and she wondered if it was possible to feel her heart break. Her brain was flooded with endless questions about how she was going to survive down here. Fear gripped her. She wasn't immortal anymore. If someone attempted to stab her now, she couldn't dissipate. She'd bleed out and die. Then her soul would forever be lost in the Underworld, run by her darling baby brother. Many wouldn't expect the blonde haired blue eyed, baby faced man to be in charge of a place that was full of such misery. The prison of souls. The place where joy ceased to exist and all that's left is agony.

Regardless of what her mother said, she couldn't help the anger in her heart that threatened to spill over at what her father had done. It was one thing to come down to Earth and play with the humans. It was another thing to banish her, strip her powers, and make her the one thing she hated most in the world. She would never be able to return home to her family, and that thought alone sent a wave of hopelessness surging through her. It was then, in that moment, she vowed to find a way back into Verus, and give her father what was coming to him. There was nothing sweeter than the nectar of revenge.

She rubbed her face and slipped on her worn shoes before making her way to the mirror and wash basin on the opposite wall before her. She gathered a handful of cold water and splashed it on her face, hoping to wake herself from this bad dream. She patted her face with a dry towel and gasped when she looked at herself in the mirror.

Her signature blood-red eyes were gone.

6

Theron had slept terribly, and his body felt horrid from the combination of poor rest and pain from his unfortunate encounter with that *thing*. With that creature who could bring even the strongest men to their knees with just a sprinkle of the onyx powder that seemed to flow from her fingertips. After the effects of the dust wore off, he came down from the cliff, fell into his bed fully dressed, and didn't even bother to shower beforehand. He had not felt this exhausted in a long time. Even from the many wars he'd served in for his village. Usually, he could hunt and train for three days straight and not feel this badly. He tried not to take it as a sign that he was getting too old, and his body was becoming unforgiving when he pushed it too far.

A knock at the door summoned him from his thoughts, and he groaned before slowly getting up to answer the door. Before him stood Gerald, his trusted Second in Command, who had led the men on the cliff yesterday against the witch.

"You look like hell, Theron," Gerald laughed. "Let's grab

some grub at the inn, what do you say?" Gerald asked, a big, goofy smile plastered on his face.

You'd think such a giant of a man wouldn't be capable of such a smile.

Gerald was one of the only friends Theron had kept in touch with once he moved into the village just outside of the Morrian mountain range. They had trained for the Northern Wind Court's royal guard when they had opened the window for new recruits, and despite losing all of his friends when Theron had been named Captain, Gerald never left his side. He didn't very well have a choice either, being his Second in Command. The poor bastard even managed to save his life a time or two when Theron made an unfortunate judgment call.

"Sure thing, let me just wash up first," he replied, pointing behind him. "Meet you there in ten?"

"Sure thing, friend," Gerald said, clapping a hand on Theron's shoulder. He felt like his bone was breaking under the force of it. Theron winced, unable to contain the look of pain. "Oops, sorry Theron." Gerald apologized, removing his hand. "I'll see you soon."

The man doesn't know his strength.

Gerald was a gentle giant, but you wouldn't know that looking at him. He was well over six feet tall, and as wide as a tree. He could crush a grown man's windpipe with one flex of his arm. If he wasn't such a kind person on the inside, and his heart was dark, he'd be unstoppable.

It's a good thing I have him on my side.

Gerald turned to walk down the dirt pathway leading away from Theron's house, and Theron tried not to collapse back into bed as he watched Gerald until he was out of sight.

7

"Excuse me?" Aella asked, her voice barely above a whisper. That was what she'd become now: a meak little worm of a girl who whispered every time she spoke. She had become what she truly loathed.

She was standing at the counter of the inn within the human village, surrounded by empty tables and chairs. A burly man stood in front of her, cleaning out a glass mug with a rag. She assumed he ran the place, but her instincts were all over the place, and she could very well be wrong. She was surprised she knew how things worked down here at all.

"What can I do for you, darling?" He asked her, not taking his eye off the glass he was cleaning meticulously. She gulped, unsure what she would need to say to sway this man to help her with what she needed. She didn't have any power over humans anymore. She couldn't threaten their lives or spook them with her signature disappearing act. Now she was one of them, and had to learn how to bargain.

"I'm sorry to bother you, sir," she started, nervously

shifting on her feet. "I'm new to town, and I'm looking for work. I'm afraid I have nowhere to go." She added the last bit to hopefully guilt the man into feeling sorry for her. If there was anything she could use to her advantage, it was the art of persuasion and guilt.

"Well, I am in need of a barmaid. Someone to serve the patrons, and clean up around here." he grumbled, now meeting her eyes. She hadn't noticed it before, but the man wore an eyepatch, and he was missing a couple of front teeth. His hair was jet black and thinning on the top.

She nodded to him before she replied. "That would be great, sir," she said, trying to sound grateful.

"None of that 'sir' nonsense. You can call me Jim." He said, holding his hand out for her to shake. She slowly gripped his hand, shaking it. He had a firm grip, his hand painted with callouses, and she felt as if he could break her hand if he squeezed hard enough.

"The breakfast rush starts soon. The job doesn't pay the greatest, but it's a start since you're new in town. It'll help you get to know the townsfolk and get you on your feet. It also comes with a room. You can keep the one you have now. We don't fill up often," Jim said, releasing her hand and turning back to drying the mug that she knew had to already be spotless. If she had to wager a guess, he'd been cleaning that same mug for the last hour.

"Thank you si-Jim, I really appreciate it." She said almost cheerfully. Her first day on Earth and she'd already gotten herself a job and a roof over her head. Maybe things wouldn't be so bad.

Take that, sweet father of mine.

Even in her mind, her sarcastic words had a bite to them.

Aella came behind the counter, and Jim handed her an

apron to wear. He spent the next hour going over the menu and the way he liked things to be done. She tried to retain everything he said, but it was almost overwhelming. She'd never had to remember so many things in her life. Not only that, but it's not like they had to eat in Verus. Food was an optional luxury. Jim gave her a pad and paper and showed her the kitchen behind the bar where she met Cook. Cook was even scarier looking than Jim was to her, and Jim informed her that he only responded in grunts, if he even responded at all.

"Cook, this is Aella. Aella, this is Cook."

As if to prove his claim of Cook's non-verbal language, Cook responded with a grunt and a nod in Aella's direction.

The kitchen was nothing special, dingy as she had expected it to be. Stacks of freshly cleaned plates and cups lined the walls, and several pots and pans crowded the stove. Steam was coming from one on the back burner, and in her new, weak human form she remembered she would have to eat, and that she was starving.

Is this what my life has come to? How annoying it is for me to feel emotions and human needs.

As if sensing her pathetic hunger building in her stomach, Cook ladled a thick brown liquid into a bowl and slid it her way with a grunt, as well as a piece of bread. She had never tasted human food before, but she was willing to do anything to satisfy this annoying pang in her belly. She took the spoon lying next to the bowl and started to slowly shovel the slop into her mouth. As the liquid hit her taste buds, she felt frantic, overtaken by the need for food. It felt like five seconds had passed before she was scraping the bottom of her bowl with the piece of bread, satisfied for the first time in her life by human food.

She took her empty bowl over to the sink, and rinsed it out before dusting herself off and tying her apron behind her back. Just as Jim had said, the breakfast rush was beginning to trickle in, and if she wanted to make any money and get ahead in her human life, she needed to get out there and start earning her wage. With a full belly and a good feeling, she took a deep breath, pushed on the kitchen door, and plastered a smile on to face the crowd.

EVERY DAY BEGAN THE SAME. EVERY SINGLE DAMN ONE.

Aella never had any deviation in her daily routine. She awoke every morning, washed up in her dusty, dingy closet sized room in the inn, before putting on the same dress and apron. She wore a gray bandana around her hair, and the same worn out shoes that caused her feet to ache and blister every day.

She had known her entire life that humans were weak, but being in this pathetic body only proved it to her ten fold. She got tired, hungry, and emotional easily. She had no control over how she was feeling mentally, physically, or emotionally, and it caused a seed of hatred to form for herself in her already black heart.

After preparing herself for the day, and wiping the crust from her eyes, she made her way downstairs and started to prepare the dining area for the breakfast folk. Cook was the only other living soul awake at this hour in the inn, the rest of their patrons sleeping for just a few more moments before thundering down the stairs. The breakfast rush consisted of the inn patrons and those who made their way in from the village. The mothers who were too tired to cook, or who wanted to treat their family to a good meal. Everyone loved Cook's food, and saw the indulgence in it as a special occasion.

The bell dinged above the door as Aella finished flipping the final stool down from the bar, signaling a customer, and the beginning of the morning rush. She made her way towards the front and stopped dead in her tracks. She locked eyes with the man whose life she'd held in her hands not so long ago. Now they were evenly matched, and judging by the look in his eyes and smirk on his face, he could sense it, too.

8

"Well, well, well. What do we have here?" Theron tutted, taking one look at the dark-haired beauty in front of him, and recognizing her instantly. "Pretending to be one of us now, witch?"

He would have recognized her anywhere; the woman who almost ended his life and literally held it in the palm of her hand. But there was a slight difference between the woman who had dangled him over a cliff and the woman standing in front of him now. Particularly the color of her eyes. He remembered those red eyes vividly, and had even dreamt about them while he tried to sleep last evening. They had been the color of the strawberries he used to pick on the farm. Now they were a cold, dark, brown like the color of freshly tilled dirt.

"I don't know what you're talking about," the witch stuttered, trying her best to keep up her ruse. "Can I interest you in some breakfast?"

"I don't think so," Theron said, searching for Jim. He spotted him in his usual place behind the counter, always drying the same mug. "Jim, mind if I borrow your waitress for a moment?"

"Sure, Theron. I don't see why not," Jim said innocently, not understanding the rage in Theron's voice. He hadn't even gazed up from the mug.

Theron watched as she overfilled the customer's mug in front of her with coffee, burning his hand and causing a curse to rip from his throat in the process.

"I'm so sorry!" She said apologetically, making quick work with her rag to soak up the mess. Her eyes connected with his again, and he could have sworn he saw fear there.

"After you," Theron said, gesturing towards the back room. The witch hesitantly walked in front of him. "Don't try to run. I have a feeling our fight will be better matched this time," he whispered so only she could hear, with venom lacing his words.

Theron followed behind her and shut the door, even turning the lock for dramatic effect. He whirled around and faced her, and he couldn't help but realize how small she looked in front of him now. Gone was the confidence and the arrogance she had not so long ago. Looking at her now made the encounter by the cliff feel like a figment of his imagination.

"Cut the innocent nonsense." He snapped, crossing his arms over his chest, and refusing to let his guard down, no matter how sad and pathetic she may look. He wouldn't let himself fall for it. "I know who you are, witch. You can't fool me, and I won't let you fool the patrons into thinking you're good and innocent. We all know your heart is as cold and bitter as a winter's night."

Theron slowly inched closer to her, closing the distance between them. He was so close to her, he could feel the body heat emitting from her. He was close enough that if she looked up and into his eyes, he'd feel her breath on his face. He couldn't help but wonder what her lips would feel like. What they'd taste like. He smelled lavender and coffee, and it was a strange yet satisfying combination.

Get it together, Theron. What are you thinking? Remember who she is.

He subtly shook his head, shaking away thoughts of her lips and the way she smelled before he spoke again. "I don't know what your game is, but you need to put an end to it."

"I'm not playing any game," she said, her voice quiet and her tone gentle despite his anger. It sent a shock wave through him. He didn't think she had a gentle bone in her body. This was all very strange to him. "This is who I am, now. Unfortunately." She said the last word under her breath like it was the worst thing to ever happen to her.

"What do you mean, unfortunately?" He asked, refusing to back down from this fight. "Don't even think about lying to me or I'll gut you like a fish."

"Well, that's rude of you. A little violent don't you think?" She said, crossing her arms over her chest and rolling her eyes, a little fire back to her words. He was beginning to see the sass in the woman he knew before she became what she was now. "You really want to know? The man who almost murdered me?"

"Oh, we are going to point fingers at who tried to murder who?" He laughed darkly. "You were the one with your hand around my throat!"

"Yeah yeah, whatever," she huffed. She headed towards a chair that sat in the corner of the room and crossed her right leg over her left. She still hadn't uncrossed her arms and she looked exhausted already, and the day hadn't even begun.

"Well, for starters my name isn't 'witch'. It's Aella, and I'm the Goddess of Chaos and Discord, or at least I was." she muttered before carrying on, "The afternoon we met, I went back up to the Sky and my father banished me here. As a human. Forever. I can never return or be with my family again. I'm stuck here. With no powers and weak as a twig. I'll be here living out my mortal lifespan until I'm dust in the wind."

Theron couldn't help the laughter that bubbled from his throat. Justice had been served, and this woman was finally getting what she deserved. After all the years of torment she had caused others, now it was time for her to suffer. But there was a thought in the back of his mind that wondered if her living on Earth would cause him to suffer as well. Now he had to see her and refrain from killing her. And he knew he'd get tired of holding back eventually.

"May I ask what's so funny? Is your tiny human brain having a hard time comprehending the truth about the rumors surrounding myself and my family?" Aella said, rage and annoyance filling her features. Such a small, meek woman now, the look did nothing to him anymore. She was vulnerable, and mortal. He would never have to fear her again, and neither would any of the others who called the village their home.

"I've never had any doubt, witch. It's just funny how quickly karma seems to deal its hand to those who deserve it," he said proudly, happy that the God of Fate was finally listening to the prayers of his people. "Don't forget you also have a tiny human brain now.'

He had no doubt that the rumors of the God and Goddesses were true. The woman standing in front of him was proof of that, especially since she'd just admitted it. No longer would they have any ounce of doubt. He'd always believed, and he was grateful to have never doubted it himself.

"My brother has a funny way of showing his love to you silly humans," Aella said, rolling her eyes, and standing up once more before him. "Since my father wants to take my powers, it's only fair I expose our existence to you pesky humans. What is he going to do to me now? Kill me? It would be a relief to be ripped from this sad body."

They both stood in silence for a moment in the pantry of the kitchen, only quick glances being passed between them. As if they were trying to decide what to do next. What the next move was going to be. He knew what he wanted to do, but he didn't want to stain Jim's clean floors with crimson blood.

"So, what is it going to be, human? Will you save my father the trouble and kill me yourself?" Aella asked as if reading his mind, looking him square in the eyes, her chin held high and the fear gone from her eyes, replaced only by fire. He wondered how good of a fight she'd even be able to give him anymore now that her powers were depleted.

"You'll pay for all of the pain you've brought to the inhabitants of this village, and your blood will spill by my hand, but today is not that day, witch. I think your soul deserves to rot away in this body for a little longer. I won't satisfy you by taking your pain away."

Theron could see the rage in her eyes at his words, before she turned around, made her way out the door, and took plates of hot food from the window. Did she expect him to feel sorry for her? To do her a favor after all the pain she caused?

Theron made his way to the counter and the plate of food

that was still thankfully warm. Aella walked back behind the counter after she tended to her tables, and he dug his fork into his own plate of food before him. She was avoiding eye contact with him, and he couldn't help the chuckle under his breath that escaped him.

She turned around and gave him a sinister glare but there was no fire behind it. She raised her eyebrow at him in silent question.

"Do you think I should feel sorry for you? That I should put you out of your misery after all the chaos you've caused my people?"

Aella didn't respond, as if she was tired of fighting already, and only turned her back on him and got back to serving the inn's patrons. Theron didn't feel an ounce of pity for her in that moment, and he knew in his heart he never would.

9

It had been weeks since Aella had been banished to life in the village, working at the inn. She had to get used to this life now. It was all she was ever going to know. It was all her future would ever entail.

Theron had been in the inn multiple times a week, always in the morning, and she hated to admit it but she had gotten used to him as well. But she'd rather die than ever admit that to him. Every morning it was the same routine between them. She would take his order and he would act like the happiest man in the entire realm to see her still alive and stuck in this weak body. This morning was no different between the two of them.

"Good morning! How's my favorite witch?" Theron asked, a sarcastic smile lacing his lips. The same fake one he used every time he addressed her. She knew he had happiness in his heart when he saw her, however. Because he knew she was still a prisoner, and the only way out was death. Her life was in his hands, because she didn't have it in her to take her own life. She'd just have to be patient and wait for the day he finally decided to end her suffering.

"Same as usual, measly human?" Aella asked, barely sparing him a glance as she wrote down his order on her notepad and put it in the window for Cook.

Aella didn't wait for him to reply before she left from behind the counter to attend to her other tables. He made it a point to sit right in front of her at the bar every morning. To make sure she saw him. It was as if he was reminding her of his promise. That one day he'd spill her blood. But it was also a constant reminder for her of how weak she'd become. It was as if he was taunting her, and how fragile she'd become.

Theron also took joy in the fact that Aella was a terrible waitress. She often wondered if her patrons gave her tips because they felt sorry for her, not because she was good. She constantly dropped plates, spilled drinks, customers rarely got their food without some incident, if they were even the proper orders to begin with. It didn't make it any better that she'd look at his face and his devilish smirk and want to punch his teeth out. He distracted her, and she got nothing good out of it in return.

But all things considered, even though Aella was potentially tormenting her patrons, they were still incredibly kind. It baffled her that people could have kindness in their heart for a stranger, and a bad-mannered stranger at that. She often cursed loudly when she fumbled with her work, and she wasn't always the nicest first thing in the morning. It was just another surprise to her about the humans. She learned more and more about them every day. Maybe they were stronger than she gave them credit for.

Aella stood in front of Theron where he was seated at the counter, looking strangely like Jim, as she polished a mug repeatedly even though it was already clean.

When Theron truly stopped and looked at Aella, he could tell her eyes were beginning to glaze, and he felt a twinge of pity in his chest. He shouldn't, but he couldn't help it. He never thought he would feel anything but hate in his heart for her. After all the pain and misery she caused him and his entire village, here he was feeling something in his heart for her. He had always helped those who had less than he. It was who he was. Even to those with darkness in their hearts. He knew how miserable she was here, and how badly she wanted her old life back. He couldn't help the thought that popped into his head. The traitorous thought that he shouldn't speak out loud, especially to this chaos maker, but it came out anyway.

"Do you know how to get back up to the, what did you call it? 'The Sky'?" He asked, wishing he'd bit his own tongue off instead. But it was too late now. There was no turning back. He couldn't unring the bell, and take back his question.

"Yes, I know the back way in. My father rules over the Sky. It's my duty to know all entrances and exits to Verus. Why do you ask, human?"

"You can't really call me human now without insulting yourself," he laughed, unable to help himself. He huffed a sigh and continued, "Because I think I know a way to get your powers back."

"What?!" She bellowed loudly, standing straight up and almost dropping the mug from her grip, causing several people to look up from their meals. "What do you mean?" She asked, her voice significantly lower after noticing the eyes on her. "How could you possibly know how to get my powers back? I never considered the possibility that my Father would take them away to begin with. So I never had a back up plan for this." She sat the mug and washrag down on the counter and began to pace back and forth, which irritated him. He walked around to the back of the counter and grabbed her arms and stopped her in front of him.

"I have some of your dust in a bottle at my house. We could sneak up to the Sky, use it on your father, and force him to give your powers back. I know what your dust can do. It cripples anyone it comes into contact with. Trust me, I know from experience," he chuckled, although nothing about his own experiences was funny.

I can't believe I'm doing this. I can't believe I'm giving her this idea.

Aella could just as easily use her dust on him if she so truly pleased. But then she'd have none left, and would be right back to square one. Only she could regenerate more of the dust, and without her powers it was impossible.

"There's no way you'd do this for me without payment in return," she said, her eyes still locked on his. For a moment he got lost in the depth of her eyes. It was as if he was swimming in a pool full of rich coffee, and he was thankful in that moment that he was an avid caffeine lover. He almost didn't hear her when she spoke again. "What is your price?"

He thought about it for a moment. Truly thought about it and tried to think about what he wanted most in this world. He considered what would be most helpful to him, and not just himself, but the village, as well. He couldn't just think of himself with a decision this big. Then, just as the other thought had hit him before, so did this one.

"I want two things. Which I feel is only fair, considering all the chaos and havoc you've wrought. This is a big deal, plus you tried to kill me," he said, holding up a finger before she could interject. " First, leave my village alone forever. We gain peace from your torment. That means quit your job, pack up whatever things you may have, and go plant your roots somewhere else if this doesn't work out. If, by some chance, it does, you still must stay away. If you can't promise this, I won't help."

"Fine, done." She said easily, as if it took no thought at all.

"Second, I want powers. I want to be able to defend this village against anything."

He watched her jaw drop to the floor, and wondered if he'd overstepped his bounds. But he didn't care. This is what she owed him.

10

owers? This man wanted powers?

Of all the things Theron could have possibly asked for, this was what he wanted in return? Not an unlimited amount of money, or food, or resources for his village, but instead he wanted to be able to wield powers of his own.

Aella wanted to laugh at how insane he must be to consider helping her. Especially after everything she'd done. Though she supposed it could be worse. She hadn't burned down his village... yet. But she couldn't give him powers. Only her father could give someone powers. But he would only be manipulated enough to grant one favor. Let alone a favor for a human. But did Theron have to know that? A devious seed of a plan began to develop in her mind, and she couldn't help but water it and make it grow.

"Alright human, I guess it's a deal." She held her hand out and shook his hand and sealed the deal with him. He was a fool, and he'd find out soon enough just how big of a mistake he'd made.

Aᴇʟʟᴀ ʟᴇꜰᴛ ᴛʜᴇ ʀᴏᴏᴍ ᴀɴᴅ ᴛᴏʟᴅ Jɪᴍ ꜱʜᴇ ᴡᴀꜱ ɢᴏɪɴɢ ᴛᴏ ʙᴇ ᴛᴀᴋɪɴɢ the next few days off, and that she'd be back in several days. He didn't seem to buy that she was taking time away to visit her family, if his grumble was any indication. She went into her small room to pack her things but realized she had nothing to pack. The way up to the Sky wasn't far, a day or two on foot, if that.. She was thankful for this. She was finished with being in the human realm, although it had been less than a month. She was tired of this frail body. She was tired of being *tired*. She turned around, took one last look at her cramped inn room, and walked out the way she came. Theron was waiting surprisingly patiently out by the front door.

"Lead the way witch," he gestured.

"This way human," she laughed, walking towards the Morrian mountain territory, where the entrance to Verus was nestled.

They walked for two hours or so, and that alone felt overwhelming to her. Her body wasn't used to this much physical activity in a tiny, weak body. She was ready to throw in the towel already, but she couldn't allow Theron to see her as weak. They still had a long way to go before they reached the entrance of Verus, and she didn't feel like hearing his jabs the entire time. He'd never let her live it down.

But after another grueling hour of walking with one foot in front of the other, legs aching for relief, she stopped and put her hands on her knees, taking deep breaths.

"Something wrong, El?" Theron asked, a smile already lacing his features. She rolled her eyes. This is exactly what she was afraid of.

"El?" she asked, just now getting her breathing under control, but hearing that nickname almost caused her to lose her breath all over again. A wave of nostalgia crashed over her, and all she could think about was home. Nobody had called her that since Pierce. It was a bittersweet feeling hearing it ring in her ears.

"Would you prefer witch?" he asked, laughing and bringing his water canteen to his lips.

"You don't have to call me anything at all," she said, standing upright and taking the water canteen from him before bringing it to her own lips. The water felt cool as it washed down her throat, and she wanted to drink all of it right then and there. But then they'd have none for later, and there wasn't a river in sight. Not until they got to the passage to the Sky anyway. She handed his canteen back to him before stretching her arms above her head.

"You ready to stop for the night?" He asked, their fingertips brushing briefly. She tried to ignore the zing of electricity it sent up her arm. She knew he could walk for a thousand miles and not break a sweat. He was doing this for her. She must have made it more obvious than she intended that she was already exhausted.

"Sure. What can I do to help?" She asked as he got the tent out of his bag and worked to get it set up.

"You can get firewood while I set up the tent," Theron offered, not taking his eyes off the tent canvas. She looked at the surrounding trees, having never gotten firewood in her life, but heading towards the forest anyway.

Aella took in the sights and the sounds around her. The

whistling of the tree branches, the singing of the birds as the sun began to sink. The crunch of the dry leaves beneath her feet. She saw several fallen branches and picked them up and placed them in her arms. Before she knew it her arms were heavily filled with the dry wood for the warm fire she could already imagine in her mind.

She made her way back into the clearing where Theron had finished setting up their sleeping quarters for the night. It wasn't as big as she thought it would be, and when she dropped the firewood next to the firepit, she peered through the open tent flap. There were two sleeping mats inside, pushed incredibly close together. Just seeing the closeness of where they'd both be laying their heads down for the night made her belly do a flip. They'd had a counter between them before, but now there was no barrier.

"You hungry?" Theron asked, pulling out two pieces of bread, and a can of beans, along with a pot to cook them over the fire.

"Starving," Aella laughed, taking a seat on a log Theron had pulled next to the fire pit that they could sit on. She watched him as he cooked, and it wasn't anything complex, but it was still one of the kindest things anyone had ever done for her. She'd never had to worry about eating before, and she had to learn very quickly that Cook wouldn't save her any food and she'd have to snag herself what she could before it was gone. But here Theron was, the man who despised her, preparing her a meal.

The fire crackled between them as he handed her a bowl of warm beans and a piece of bread. She blew on each spoonful, careful not to burn the roof of her mouth with how desperate she was to devour the grub. Silence stretched between them, and the only sounds were the insects chirping in the evening air, and the sounds of the owls calling to one another.

Before she knew it, it was time to get some rest, and she couldn't say she was upset about it. Her body was angry at her for pushing it too hard today, and she hoped a good night's rest would fix everything. With the impending visit to the Sky , she'd need all the strength she could muster. She needed her wits about her.

Aella looked to Theron, and found his eyes already on her.

"Well, I'm going to head to bed for the night." he said, after clearing his throat.

"I'll be right in," she replied, feeling heat rise to her cheeks. She wasn't sure when the switch had happened, but she found herself able to tolerate this one particular mortal's existence.

She didn't want to begin to understand what it could mean.

II

As Theron pulled back the tent flap, he tried to push the image of Aella next to the fire out of his mind. The way the light illuminated her milky white skin. The way her once red eyes shone brightly, like there wasn't a drop of evil within her entire being.

He couldn't let himself forget what she had done. Not only to him, but to his people. He couldn't allow himself to get lost in the way she looked, and forget about how ugly her soul was on the inside.

He quickly changed into his fleece pajamas, and laid his head down on his pillow before she could come in. For all he knew, she was long gone by now, having run away to escape their bargain. He doubted very much that she'd actually follow through with her end of the deal, and he wouldn't die in the process at her hand. She may be mortal now, but she was still incredibly cunning.

A vicious little thing.

Speaking of the Goddess herself, mortal or not, she made her way in the tent and into her own bed beside him. His back was to her, but regardless, he could still see her and her every move in his mind. He had gotten used to the way she moved, how certain emotions made her face look. It was annoying how much space she was taking up in his mind.

THERON AWOKE IN THE MIDDLE OF THE NIGHT, AND SHIVERS RACKED his body. He hadn't anticipated how cold the autumn air would be. And due to that, he hadn't packed any extra bedding. All he had packed for himself and Aella was a thick blanket. He turned over and saw that she was still fast asleep, but she wouldn't be for long. Because her body was also shaking from the cold.

He rolled to his back and tried to ponder what to do. He could give her his blanket, but then he'd freeze himself. He refused to take hers. So he did the one thing that made logical sense. He rolled onto his side, and gathered her into his arms. It took a few moments but her shivers subsided, and a small, pleasant sigh escaped her lips. She looked so peaceful when she was asleep. Her face was relaxed and empty of the scowl it usually contained. She looked truly and unequivocally human. Her small form fit so perfectly against him, as if they were two puzzle pieces coming together.

It would forever blow his mind how such a small, innocent looking woman could have such a fiery heart and soul. He couldn't help the rise of emotions that seized his heart. How he never could imagine anyone else belonging in his arms.

Damn it. I cannot fall for her.

But damn it if I was to deny I was.

12

The first thing Aella noticed when she woke up the next morning was the rays of the sunlight shining directly in her eyes through the crack in the tent flaps.

The second thing she noticed was the large set of muscular arms surrounding her middle. Her eyes widened as she processed the fact that it was the mortal that despised her, currently holding her close and whose breath she felt on her neck. Not only that, but she could feel Theron's hard length pressing against her backside. Heat rose up her neck and cheeks before she could stop it.

Impressive for a mortal.

Aella also had to process the fact that a small part of her was savoring this moment. All sexual thoughts filling her head aside. It was nice to be laying in a strong man's arms. Feeling protected and safe for once in her life by someone that wasn't herself. She had lived every second of her life on edge. Always worried that the chaos she caused would come back to bite her one day. She was right to think so, especially considering everything that had happened in just a few short weeks.

As slow and careful as Aella could, she worked to remove herself from Theron's hold so she could get out of the tent and stretch, and get a taste of the crisp morning air. A sleepy groan escaped him as she moved his arm, but as far as she could tell, he rolled over and quickly went back to sleep. It surprised her that she was up before him, considering he was a warrior and all. Weren't they engineered to be morning people?

Aella felt the grass tickle her skin, the morning dew soaking the soles of her feet and the padding of her toes. She stretched her arms fully above her head, and leaned gently from side to side to alleviate the tension in her muscles from a long journey and a stiff cot.

She lowered her eyes and took a deep breath in through her nose, and could taste the moisture in the air that was an omen of the rainfall to come. She could hear the songs of the birds from the forest, and the chatter of the leaves as they sang in the breeze. She had never appreciated nature as much when she was a Goddess. She was beginning to realize she took a lot of things for granted when she was a Goddess. A lot of things that may have seemed simple, but were in fact magical in their own right. It was something she'd miss when she got her powers back, but she vowed to be more mindful of her surroundings. Stop and smell the roses every once in a while.

"Ready to go?" Theron's voice came from behind her. Her eyes flew open and she startled at the sound of his greeting. When she turned around, he had already dismantled the tent and packed their bags. How long had she been in her own little world of nature?

"I suppose so," she replied, grabbing her bag from his outstretched hand. She didn't mention the embrace they had shared this morning, and he didn't seem to be inclined to bring it up either. Without another word, he turned and made his way to the north and towards the entrance to Verus. She had been steering him in the right direction, and let him lead since his steps were much faster than hers, and she tended to lag behind. They had gotten most of the traveling out of the way yesterday, so there wasn't much ground left to cover now.

They walked in silence for some time, the only sounds were the branches that broke beneath their feet and the dry leaves that crunched from fallen trees in preparation for winter. It was just a few weeks into the autumn months, where the air had a bite to it, and the colors were vibrant. Aella had always enjoyed coming down during this time of year more than any other. She despised the sweltering heat, and the frigid cold accompanied by snow. So spring and autumn were what she favored.

Aella stared at the ground while she walked, but a hint of yellow caught her attention from the corner of her eye, and with a quick intake of air as she realized what they had stumbled upon, she ran.

13

This woman was going to cause him to have an early visit to his grave.

It wasn't enough that she had held Theron by the throat over a cliff, one twitch of her fingers and he'd have been splattered on the rocks below. Alas, the beautiful dark haired woman, who it seemed was chaos even as a mortal, was making a run towards Gods knew what.

Theron had been leading the way towards Verus, and he had heard her sharp inhale before he turned and saw her disappearing over the hill to their left.

"Hey!" He yelled loudly towards her, already beginning to run after her so he could catch her before she escaped. At first, he assumed she was running away before she could live up to her end of their bargain, but once he caught sight of what awaited at the bottom of the hill, he somewhat understood why she was running. But it was made more abundantly clear when she turned around and gave him a playful smirk. As if she *wanted* him to chase her. Chase her right into the field of tall, fully bloomed sunflowers before them.

Theron stopped, having lost sight of Aella and her black mane of hair running wildly through the flowers. He scanned around, knowing that without her powers there's no way she could have vanished into thin air.

"Oof!" A force came out of nowhere and knocked the wind out of him, causing him to fall straight into the dirt beneath his feet. He landed on his back and when he looked back up, it was Aella's face staring back at him, her body weight holding him down. Her cheeks were flushed from the run, and her breath tickled his skin. She had a sparkle in her eyes and she was laughing so freely, he noticed once he realized that she had tackled him in a playful way and not aggressively.

Theron looked into those beautiful, chocolate brown eyes and he felt an ache in his chest that he didn't know how much longer he could deny. He took her face in his hands, unable to help himself, and she stopped laughing instantly. He tucked a piece of stray hair behind her ear, and his eyes traveled down to her very kissable lips. What was the worst thing that would happen if he kissed her?

Consequences be damned.

ONE MOMENT AELLA WAS LOOKING INTO THERON'S EYES, AND THEN he grabbed her face, his callous hands rough and warm against her smooth skin. And then she must have fallen asleep because there was no way that this wasn't a dream.

Theron's lips crashed against hers, kissing her into abandon. As if he was starving his entire life and had now just gotten a taste of her lips and never wanted to go without it again. His lips were soft against hers, and she moaned into his mouth at how good they felt against hers. He pulled away just for a moment to search her eyes for any chance of regret, and he wouldn't find any. This time she brought her lips to his, and he sighed against her, before trailing his tongue down the seam lips as a request that she was more than happy to oblige.

Their tongues intertwined, and a shot went to her core that she hadn't felt in many years. She had sworn herself off from men for the longest time, tired of the same thing over and over. But now with Theron, she was willing to make a surprising exception. She knew she wasn't alone in her feelings of need with the hard length of Theron pressing against her belly. She could have taken him right then and there. If he would have made any move towards it, she would have let him.

Consequences be damned.

But Aella couldn't help but remember who she was, where they were, and where they were going. She knew she had to put a stop to this. She couldn't let herself have him. She didn't deserve someone as good as him.

Trying to be as casual as she could about it, she broke away from him and rolled off him and onto her back. She gazed up into the sky, watching the clouds as they rolled by. She could feel his eyes on her, his gaze burning a hole straight to the center of her being, but she just breathed deeply and smiled to the sky.

"What do you think that one looks like?" Theron asked, and it took her a moment to realize he was pointing at a cloud in the sky.

"A sky dragon, most definitely." Aella laughed, only part

way joking. Sky dragons were very sneaky, stealthy creatures. She wouldn't be surprised if she saw one in the sky. They were hard to see unless you knew what you were looking for.

"Oh. I was going to say a horse," Theron frowned, before looking to her and bursting into laughter. She could have laid here with him, in this moment, forever. She felt a pit begin to form in her stomach, as she began to realize that she was perhaps, and impossibly, falling in love with this mortal.

14

Theron laid in the sunflower field with Aella for what felt like an eternity, watching the clouds. Their hands just a centimeter apart, almost touching. They were so close he could feel her warmth, and he swore he could feel the electricity zipping from her fingertips to his own. He had never felt such a connection to someone. Granted, it had been several years since he'd allowed himself to have a relationship, too busy focused on protecting his village. He'd honestly believed lately that he would have grown old by himself. Not that he ever would have had an issue with it.

Until now.

Until he caught himself realizing that he was falling in love with the Goddess of Chaos.

Consequences be damned.

EVENTUALLY THEY BOTH CAME TO TERMS WITH THE FACT THAT THEY couldn't lay in a field of flowers forever. Despite how much they would have liked to. In a moment where they had no worries. Theron wasn't panicked about protecting his village. Not that he was anyway, knowing he'd left a very capable Gerald behind. And Aella wasn't trapped and over-thinking in her mind about her lack of powers and fragility. It was just the two of them, and the golden sunflowers rustling in the wind.

Theron broke first, pushing himself off the ground before turning back towards Aella and extending his hand.

"Ready to go?" He asked, his hair tousled and messy from the way he was laying on the ground. She smiled to herself, liking this carefree look to him. But she wouldn't tell him that.

"I suppose," she said, placing her hand in his. She couldn't help but realize how perfect their hands fit together and how good it felt for their skin to be touching.

She grabbed her pack and silently said goodbye to the sunflowers and their shared moment.

"After you mortal," Aella said, a teasing tone to her voice, pointing towards the north, where they'd soon find the Sky's entrance. Where everything would change. He laughed at her silly nickname for him before leading the way once more. As they walked, she tried to ignore the feeling of dread that began to grow. For once in her life, she was beginning to imagine a simple existence. One without chaos.

It wasn't long before they came towards the cliff edge, so close to the doorway, and memories of her almost killing Theron came back to her. She couldn't help but feel so many silly human emotions today and right now she felt guilt. Something she had never felt before. She had been feeling emotions she never knew existed in her short time living amongst the humans. The burden that human's carried, always having to juggle so many complicated sensations at once. She never knew.

"Hey Theron?" she asked, while they both gazed towards the edge of the cliff. He looked at her, those beautiful eyes peering into her soul. "I'm sorry for almost taking your life."

"Hmph, you wouldn't have been able to manage it," he said, his signature smirk on his lips. "Where to now? You're not going to push me over the cliff, are you?"

He chuckled as he gazed at her, but she could see the worry that flitted over his eyes. It's as if he had no idea the admiration she now carried in her heart for him.

"What? That kiss wasn't enough to prove I no longer wish to take your life?" She laughed. "No human, I don't plan to push you over. This is the way to the Sky."

She gestured towards the sky, where even as a human she could see the change in the clouds where the portal led to her home. Well, she supposed she was used to it by now, but any other human's blind eye couldn't see it if they tried. She grabbed his hand and began to lead him toward the portal. He looked like she had bitten him when she grabbed his hand. As if he still didn't quite fully trust her. That maybe he did perhaps think she would indeed throw him over the cliff.

"Don't worry Theo, I just need to hold on to you and make sure you don't get lost in the clouds."

"Theo huh? What happened to mortal?"

Her face turned cherry red at her slip up and the fact that she had a decent nickname for him now.

Aella shook off the feeling of embarrassment and closed her eyes. She began to feel the familiar suction into the portal, and before she knew it, she felt her feet hit the pavement of her house's porch. She smiled, because she had pictured her location, and it had worked perfectly.

Even as a mortal I've still got it.

She had hoped that she wouldn't end up in front of the gates. The guards would have taken her and she would have been killed by her father instantly. He wouldn't have hesitated. She needed the element of surprise on her side and, for once, things were working in her favor. Theron's eyes were wide, and she realized he'd never seen the Sky before. She hesitated to roll her eyes, but then remembered how brilliant it must look to his human eyes. She'd seen it a thousand times before, but this was his first. It took all but a moment of watching the awe in his expression for her to realize she liked watching him appreciate the beauty of her home.

The polished, silver gates and the way the willow tree branches swayed in the wind. The way the sun shone on the surface of the pool of Eternity. The way the brick pathway sounded underneath their boots. She breathed in a big gulp of Verus air, and she could feel the peace spread through every extremity. She had become so used to the air on the ground that breathing in the air on top of the clouds felt like she'd never breathed air before. She spared a glance at Theron and knew he was feeling the same way. Except he really had never experienced something like this before.

Aella tried to see through the eyes of the mortal standing beside her, and take in the environment and the small, quaint house that stood before them. Aella's house wasn't the biggest, or the most glamorous in Verus, but she wasn't upset about it in the slightest. The one story dwelling was made out of light gray stone, with enough windows that she only needed a lamp at night time. Despite her job description, the decor inside was light in color. Whites, grays, dark greens littered everything. The carpet was soft and plush beneath her toes and it was why she'd had it installed.

Aella could see the gears working in Theron's head. As if he was taking in everything around him since they walked through her front door and using it to make further judgements about her. As if he could read into her soul by the way she decorated her home.

"Your home is beautiful," Theron said, his voice filling the quiet. "How many books do you have?" He asked, his eyes searching the wall of bookshelves in her living room.

"So many I think I've lost count," she replied, fiddling with her fingers to distract from the strange feelings of nerves she felt in her belly. "I love to read."

"I would never have thought the Queen of Chaos liked to read," he laughed, fingers gently swiping over the many titles.

"It's Goddess of Chaos," Aella replied. "But I guess I qualify as a Queen somewhere."

"So what's next?" Theron wondered, turning to face her.

"Now, we plan," Aella responded, a look of mischief gracing her face.

15

Theron had never seen anything like Verus in his life. He'd been in the Morrian territory and seen the mountains. The lake that was at the end of the river that flowed through it. The evergreen tree patches littered throughout. But this was an entirely different experience. An entirely different world. And with all of this beauty surrounding him, he was only able to focus on the beautiful woman before him. The house she had made her home and all of the personal touches she'd given it. He felt like he learned a lot about her just from looking around. From scanning the titles on her shelves.

He was beginning to realize that there was more to the Goddess of Chaos than met the eye. That she wasn't cold and dead inside. That there was a part of her that was warm, and kind. That saw the beauty in things. Who needed to escape from reality with a good book sometimes, too.

Maybe Theron had been too quick to judge her when he first saw her in the Inn. Maybe he'd even been too quick to judge her when she held his life in her hands. Maybe Chaos was all she knew. And in some weird, twisted way, it gave her the joy he found in being a warrior.

Aella laid out a map on her dining room table of the Temple where her parents were located.

"My parents have never changed anything about the layout of their house nor the way it's guarded. When you're King of the Sky, and an immortal being, you think nothing can happen to you and nobody can touch you." Aella smiled before continuing on. "Enter me. Pissed off, revenge filled daughter whose middle name is Chaos and whose companion is a mere mortal who wants powers.

"There are twelve guards in total in the entire building. Six on the inside, and six on the outside. They change position and rotate every six hours. At night time, they lose two guards so there's only ten total. Our best bet is to go after dinner time. He'll be less pissed off and we both have a better chance of getting what we want."

"So what do we do with our time until tomorrow evening?" Theron questioned.

"Well human, luckily for you, you get to spend just a little bit more time with me," Aella replied with a smile playing on her lips. "You hungry?"

"Very hungry witch," Theron answered, an answering smile gracing his own lips.

"Are you asleep?" Aella asked, peering into the doorway of the room where Theron was laying in bed.

She'd cooked him an authentic Verus meal. She'd even

caught the fish she'd cooked from the lake next to her home. She'd snuck to her neighbor's backyard, in their garden, and grabbed a handful of herbs and potatoes, as well as enough food to stock her fridge for a couple days. It had been so long since she'd cooked her own meal. She loved cooking . Even though she didn't eat out of necessity, something about preparing the ingredients and enjoying the fruits of her labor made it that much more enjoyable.

But she could get used to more meals like this. More laughs like this. More time like this. It was blissful and peaceful. Maybe it was the wine going to her head, but if she spent the rest of her days like this, she wouldn't complain. Who was she? She had never felt this way before. She'd done an entire one-eighty in the time she'd met Theron and the small amount of time she'd spent with him.

I suppose that's what love does to you.

Wait. Love? Was this love? Did she love this mortal? She shook the thought from her head and tiptoed into the room.

"Theron?" Aella whispered loudly.

"What?" Theron's muffled voice filled the space. She could barely see in the dark, the moonlight leaking onto the bed from the large windows the only light in the room. He lifted his head out from under the pillow and she could see the mess of his hair and his back muscles flexing as he did so.

"I can't sleep," she said, tiptoeing her way slowly towards his bed. He flopped his head down on his pillow and sighed loudly. She made her way to the opposite side of the bed and lifted up the covers and shimmed her way underneath them. It was crazy for her to think about the fact that she was on such good terms with Theron that she was capable of getting under the covers with him without fear or embarrassment.

"Are you going to miss me?" Aella asked jokingly, hearing his series of groans as she fluffed the pillows behind her head.

"Oh yes, most definitely," Theron said sarcastically, admitting defeat and propping himself up on the headboard. He let out a deep sigh before he continued on.

"It will be strange not being on my toes every second of every day," he admitted. "I've been wondering if I even should ask for powers considering the fact that you won't be coming back."

Aella couldn't help but feel surprised at his confession. Her eyes met his in the ray of moonlight, and she tried to decipher what he could possibly be thinking.

"So what are you still doing here?" Aella asked, not sure if she truly wanted to know the answer. And not sure if she'd help him go home if he asked.

"You haven't figured it out yet?" His eyes searched her face, before landing on her lips for a brief moment. "I'm here for you, Aella."

She couldn't fight it anymore. She couldn't fight the feelings that were swirling in her heart anymore.

Consequences be damned.

Aella crashed her lips to his, without a single care in the world. She felt a zing of electricity go right to her core, and she knew they'd both held back in the field of sunflowers, but hoped that wasn't the case anymore. If she was never going to see him again when this was all over, she was going to make the most of their time together.

His lips seemed hesitant at first against hers, but it took him all of two seconds before he moved against her, letting out a groan of pleasure into her mouth. Even though it was her who initiated the first move, she didn't stay in control for long. He towered over her, running his hands up and down her side, before one of his hands landed around her throat. He gave it a little squeeze, and she moaned in response. Never before had she allowed herself to be dominated, especially in the bedroom, but with Theron? He made her feel all kinds of things she never had before.

With one of his hands squeezing her throat, the other traveled down and cupped one of her breasts and gave it a rough squeeze, before rolling her nipple between his fingertips. She threw her head back, groaning in pleasure just from the tormentingly light touches, having not even traveled anywhere near the wetness between her thighs.

"You're losing control already? Darling, I've barely started," Theron purred in a gravely tone.

She met his eyes and smiled, his eyes were full of flaming lust and ecstasy. He took one thin strap of her nightgown and moved it to the side, letting her breasts out into the cool night breeze. Theron laughed lightly before bringing his mouth to her bare breast and working his tongue around her peak. It had been too damned long since she'd given into her desires, but the wait was paying off in this moment.

Aella took one of her hands and ran it through Theron's hair, pushing him closer into her chest, the other traveled down to his impressive length straining against his boxers. She began to stroke him through his undergarments, and in response he gave her nipple a nibble.

She squeaked , causing a laugh to come from Theron against the mouthful of her breast. He let go, and traveled his hands down, down, down, until he was where she wanted him most. They weren't speaking, but they didn't need to. Everything that needed to be said was in their movements.

"Lay back for me baby," Theron said, gently pushing her onto her back, and sliding up her nightgown.

"Fuck," he hissed, discovering she wasn't wearing any underwear underneath her nightgown. He nestled between her thighs, a hand on either one, and she could feel his hot breath on her core.

He took one of his fingers and glided it through her soaking wet cunt.

"Is all of this for me?' He asked, slowly and painfully teasing her.

"Theron," she begged, not knowing how much more she could take.

"Say my name again. Beg for it Aella. Beg for the mere mortal to feast on you,"

"Please, Theron," Aella whined. She'd never begged for anything in her life, but this, she would beg for.

"Mortal body or not, let me worship you as the Goddess you are," Theron said, before settling between her thighs and doing exactly that.

As his tongue worked her over, she could have sworn she saw the stars, galaxies, the whole damn universe from the pleasure he was giving. She'd never been intimate with a human before, but she knew this was no talent of just any mortal. It was the talent of Theron himself.

As he continued to move his tongue, he moved his fingers up and down her slit once more before inserting a finger and moving it quickly inside her. She felt so close to the cliff already but having even just one of his fingers inside her and his tongue on her bud was enough to make her combust.

"Theron!" She yelled, screaming his name without abandon.

"That's right Aella. Let every God and Goddess in Verus know that a mere mortal had the ability to make the Goddess of Chaos lose control." He laid on his back, and his impressive bulge tented his underwear. She wet her lips in anticipation, knowing what he was going to ask for before he even asked.

"I want to see your mouth around me baby," Theron requested, his need evident in his voice. She wasn't sure why the thought of her taking him in her mouth made her nervous, but she shook it away and proceeded to pull down his underwear and let his erection bounce free.

Aella wasted no time, gripping his thickness in her hand and stroking his shaft. He hissed in return, closing his eyes and throwing his head back in pleasure just as she had in response to him.

Before he brought his head back down, she put him in her mouth, and began to work him over. She watched him through heavy lashes as his head snapped down, his eyes roaring with sexual desire. He gripped her hair and pulled, causing a moan to escape her lips as he moved her head the way he wanted.

"I've been wondering what those lips might look like wrapped around me ever since I first saw you in the Inn," Theron said breathlessly. "You did not disappoint."

Aella smiled, before gripping him as she continued working him with her mouth.

"Aella," he hissed. His tone held a warning that he too was about to lose control. Her response was simple enough as she moved faster and faster until she felt him release into the back of her throat and he moaned her name loudly. She had barely wiped her mouth before he flipped her onto her back, and hovered over her.

"Impatient are we?" She laughed. "I didn't even know if you wanted me."

"You just stood there, in your skimpy little night gown and thought I wouldn't notice?" Theron growled, using his arms to hold himself above her, teasing her entrance with his length. "I notice everything about you."

She smiled for a moment before she gasped as he thrust himself into her, stretching her wide. She lost all sense of time and reality as he continued to pound against her flesh. She never wanted to stop feeling this. With each pump of him into her, she could feel more strings of their souls connecting. She'd never felt a connection during sex before. It was something the Gods did for fun and for pleasure, but with Theron everything was different. She could see flashes of the future they could have. The love they could share. The memories they could create. She didn't care what she had to do, she'd find a way for them to be together. She felt herself getting closer to the edge again, and she could tell by the way Theron worked his jaw and clenched his teeth that he was there with her.

"Aella," his voice again holding the same warning tone. "I'm close, baby."

"I'm right there with you, Theo." She tried to keep her voice even but the pleasure was all consuming.

He thrust into her harder and faster before she felt him release inside of her, and slow his pace. He pulled himself out of her now full entrance and fell on his back beside her.

"Wanna go again?" she asked, partly joking but mostly serious. He looked at her and laughed, before pulling her on top of him and burying himself in her once more.

THERON LAID THERE IN BED, MEMORIZING AND COMMITTING EVERY one of Aella's curves to memory. His hands tracing the lines and planes of her naked back.

"Do you ever think about giving it up for good?" Theron inquired.

"What? Being a Goddess?" Aella asked.

"Mhm," Theron hummed, his hands still taking in every inch of supple skin on her back.

"Before? Absolutely not. My life was nothing without being an all powerful Goddess with an immortal life span. But now?" Her eyes lazily drifted towards his, as if he could see the exhaustion seeping into her. "Now, I could give it up without hesitation if you asked me to."

"I'd never ask you to give up something you love," her eyes were fluttering closed as she listened to him speak.

"I'm beginning to find new things to love," she whispered, before her breathing slowed and he could tell she was deep into sleep already.

"I am too," Theron whispered back, leaning over to place a kiss on her forehead before nestling next to her and letting sleep claim him as well.

Sunlight filtered in through the windows and nearly blinded him the next morning. It took Theron a moment to gather himself and remember where he was. He peered over and saw the beautiful woman he loved laying next to him and breathed a sigh of happiness and relief. It hadn't been a dream at all.

He slowly lifted the covers off of himself and gently crept out of bed and pulled his pants over his legs. He walked into the kitchen scratching the back of his head, and opened the pantry to see what was inside. She had given him the night of his life, the least he could do was make her breakfast.

Theron pulled out eggs and breakfast meat and began to cook while whistling happily. He could get used to this. Maybe they could make something work. He could come visit her, she could come visit him. A sly, dangerous idea crept into the back of his mind.

Maybe I could leave the village in the hands of Gerald...

"Good morning," Aella's sleep filled voice greeted from behind him, pulling him from his thoughts.

"Good morning. I hope you're hungry," Theron smiled back to her, before piling her plate with food and placing it in front of her at the table.

"I'm famished," Aella replied, before grabbing her fork and digging into the meal he had prepared. She groaned with her first bite, and he couldn't help the zing that traveled down low. Her eyes popped up, seeming to realize what she'd done and she froze for a moment before they both began laughing.

Theron took his own plate and sat down next to her, shoveling food into his mouth as if he hadn't eaten in days.

"It's delicious Theron, thank you," Aella said, her plate already empty.

"Are you ready for today?" He questioned, knowing he was looking forward to, but also dreading, what the end of the day might bring. His mind was flipping back and forth about what he wanted to do, what he needed to do, and what he should do. He wanted to say forget asking for powers, and instead ask for an eternity with Aella. He needed and should, however, go along with the plan they had in place and return to his post at the village. What if he'd been reading the room wrong, and Aella wasn't feeling the same way he had been?

But he knew in his mind that wasn't true. The way he felt about her, and the way his soul sang for hers? There wasn't a shadow of a doubt that she was feeling it too.

16

After breakfast, lots of sex, followed by lunch and more sex, they'd carefully gone over their plan to invade the temple and finish what they'd come here to do. This was it. This was the evening that would change everything, for better or for worse.

Aella and Theron slowly, and with as much stealth as they could muster, made their way to the outer wall of the temple. She could hear the whistling of the guard on watch, and if she had her powers he'd be put to sleep in an instant. But they were going to have to do things the old-fashioned way.

"Oof!" The guard shouted as Theron hit him in the back of the head with the pommel of his sword. They made quick work to move his body into the bushes and out of sight from any wandering eyes. They crouched and moved quickly past the pool and to the side of her parent's home.

She took the bag of dust that Theron had given her out of her pocket, ready to use it in an instant. She knew this time of day her father usually took a post-dinner snooze. It was the only time he ever stopped and slowed down.

Aella crept on her tiptoes and avoided the windows, which only had thin curtains to cover them. She knew if she was seen, it was game over entirely. Both herself and Theron would be dead with the snap of her father's fingers. She was incredibly aware of how vulnerable she was here. She slowly opened the wooden back door, hoping with everything in her that it didn't creak. It thankfully opened without a sound, and she put a finger to her mouth to shush Theron.

They ever so slowly made their way into the living room, her father's snores filling the empty space and echoing off the walls. If everything she knew was correct, her mother would be upstairs reading a novel. It was where she had gotten her love of reading from.

She snuck ever so slowly up behind her father, his head resting on the arm of the couch. She looked at his face and began to feel a sickness wash over her. She missed her father and pictured her childhood years in her mind. When she was younger, they were so close. But he had banished her without a second thought. A nagging and vicious thought in the back of her mind wondered if he'd loved her at all. Or if he'd only ever sought to control her. She reached inside the pouch of her dust and sprinkled some right on her father's face.

His nose began to crinkle and he coughed. It looked like she had sprinkled pepper on his nose, but he was in for a rude awakening. He began to gasp for air, and his eyes sprang open and she saw nothing but a black abyss staring back at her.

"Oh daddy," she purred in his ear. "You should have known I'd come back with a vengeance."

"What do you want?" he choked out, his face turning different shades from the lack of oxygen.

"I want my powers back, is what I want." she yelled as the wind began to pick up around them, throwing her hair around her face. "You should have never taken them in the first place!"

"It was for your own good!" Her father's voice boomed, despite his inability to breathe properly.

"You know nothing about what's good for me!" Aella fired back.

She could feel his life force slipping away. Only a fellow God or Goddess could kill their own kind, and it was a cardinal sin against the hierarchy. She was losing precious time, and her father was the only one who could bestow her powers back to her. If he died before that happened, her powers would die with him. Theron was silent beside her, watching the scene unfold. He didn't seem to be affected by her actions, nor was he chomping at the bit to make his own demands.

"If you know what's good for me, you'll give me back my powers." Aella made sure the venom she felt in her heart oozed into her words as she spoke.

"Fine Aella, take them!" He screamed at her, thrusting a ray of light at her. She felt the bone-crunching pain again as she was joined once more with her powers. She had never felt more alive.

"That's better," she said, snapping her fingers so a black dress slipped over her body and strappy heels adorned her feet. She finally felt like herself, again. The Goddess of Chaos, through and through. "Don't worry daddy, I'll take the pain away."

She slowly walked towards him as he spasmed in pain.

She put her hands on either side of his head, and he took one last pained gasp before he went limp. The wind died down, and her father's soul with it. She turned around to find Theron staring back at her wide-eyed, as her mother rushed in behind him.

"AELLA! What have you done?!" Her mother screamed, flinging herself over her husband's corpse. She began to wail louder than Aella ever had heard.

"Don't worry mommy, you'll join him soon," she said, and before her mother could take a moment and think about what her daughter said, she turned to ash and blew away in the wind.

"Aella?" She heard Theron's sad voice behind her, and her plan was working perfectly. She had her powers back, and she no longer had to live a sad mortal life.

But you weren't sad at all.

A battle was raging inside of her, and her heart ached not knowing which part of herself to give into.

She turned her attention again to Theron and saw fear in his eyes at what she had become. She could feel the goodness in her wanting to come back. To embrace her again just as Theron had.

"Come back to me, baby," Theron said, slowly inching closer to her. She closed her eyes, ready to turn off her Chaos. To hang it up once and for all. She hadn't lied when she told Theron she was finding other things to love.

"I'm sorry, pathetic human, but this was never going to work in your favor."

Aella's eyes flew open as she heard Theron groan in pain, before his knees hit the floor. She ran to him, catching him in her arms as blood pooled from his stomach. She looked up to see Pierce standing there, his sword in his hand and a smile on his face.

"Theron?" She cried, his eyes groggily moving between hers and searching her face. As if he was memorizing everything about her. "Theron! Stay with me! I can help you!"

She ran her hand over his wound, his blood staining her hands. She was the Goddess of Chaos. She had no way to heal him with the power she'd been given. The only people in this room who could were both dead. The irony of the situation didn't escape her.

Theron smiled weakly, seeming not at all concerned that he was dying.

"You may always be a woman of chaos, but it's what I love most about you."

"You love me?" Aella cried, remembering how desperate she had been to hear those words.

"I realized I fell in love with you when you laid on top of me in a field of sunflowers without a care in the world."

"I love you, Theron," she cried, as she could hear his heartbeat slowing. "I'll always love you."

He smiled one last time, before she watched the light drain from his eyes. It felt like someone had ripped her heart right out of her chest. This was the day her heart would die. Where her soul would shrivel and never recover from the agony of losing her lover. She sobbed over his lifeless body, hoping everyone in Verus, Earth and beyond heard her cries of anguish.

"Come on El. Let's go," Pierce said, grabbing her arm.

She looked at his hand in disgust, before slowly turning her attention towards his face. She saw a flash of fear , and it only excited her as she slipped into a place of emotionless darkness. Where she wouldn't have to feel the pain of losing Theron.

She snapped her fingers, and Pierce thudded to the ground, lifeless before her eyes. Power was radiating off of her, sparking at her fingertips. It hadn't been used and was waiting to be released. Her rage filled heart only fueled it.

She smiled, closed her eyes, and when she opened them, she watched the world she once knew and loved go up in flames around her. If she couldn't have the happiness she craved, and the man she loved, nobody else could either.

Theron had been the only man to ever love her despite all the Chaos swirling within her soul. Her parents had loved her when they could keep her Chaos locked away, but they'd never loved her for who she truly was. She was a fool to think she'd be able to change that.

She decided when her time came, and she ended her immortal life, she would die a villain and felt no shame doing so as she watched Verus turn to ash.

EPILOGUE

The sound of shackles filled the stale air of Eronder as Aella was led to her eternal prison. She had been a fool to think her brothers and sisters would let her get away with burning their home without consequences.

"We hereby banish you to an eternity in Eronder," she remembered her sister Yara, the Goddess of Fate, reading her verdict at the silly hearing they'd held in the already rebuilt Verus. That was what she got for having a sister who was the Goddess of Time. All she had to do was work her magic and everything was as it should have been. Except for Theron and her parents, that is. Only her brother, the God of Life and Death could undo what she had done, and he was a fickle bitch when it came to bringing back the dead.

They thought they had the upper hand. That they could lock her away down here and throw away the key. That they could leave her with only a wicked smile on her face, and a thirst for revenge embedded in her soul.

But they couldn't have been more wrong.

... IF YOU GAZE INTO THE ABYSS, THE ABYSS WILL SWALLOW YOU whole...

THE END

ACKNOWLEDGMENTS

I cannot believe I now have three (if you count my anthology piece/novella) books out!! Thank you for following me on this wild journey of mine, and showing my books love!

As aways, I could never do what I do without the Lord, who gives me the strength to write these and blessed me with a wild imagination to write them.

I could never do this without the support of my amazing husband who supports everything I do even if he hasn't read any of my work yet.

And last, but seriously absolutely positively not least, my amazing editor who has my heart and soul forever. Thank you for helping me bring my stories to life!

ABOUT THE AUTHOR

Kylie Vennefron, better known as Ky Venn, loves to build fantasy worlds, and send her characters on great adventures. When she's not writing, you can find her either watching Grey's Anatomy, reading a book, or spending time with her family. She enjoys being a wife, a child of God, and a mama to her daughter and two fur babies. She currently lives with her husband and child in Hamilton, Ohio.

Sign up for my newsletter below & get exclusive content, sneak peeks, and more!

ALSO BY KY VENN

Justice in Magic

Printed in the USA
CPSIA information can be obtained
at www.ICGtesting.com
JSHW022318130324
58902JS00001B/21